Katabatic

A *Constable David Maratse* novella

set in Greenland
~ Greenland Crime Stories #1 ~

by Christoffer Petersen

Don't miss the next in the series:

Container

KATABATIC

Published by Aarluuk Press

Copyright © Christoffer Petersen 2023

ISBN: 978-1-980427-10-0

www.christoffer-petersen.com

CHRISTOFFER PETERSEN

That *I* must censor
This Grief, it will rage again,
that *I* swore over the Murderer
Vengeance, which I will not restrain.

Author's translation from
EN SORG
by
LUDVIG MYLIUS-ERICHSEN (1872-1907)

Da maatte jeg betvinge
en Graad, der vilde frembrudt,
da svor jeg over Morderen
en Hævn, jeg ikke har fortrudt.

KATABATIC

Author's Note

I met Constable David Maratse in a bar in Greenland. This is his story, as much as it is mine.

CHRISTOFFER PETERSEN

Katabatic

KATABATIC

1

The man was already dead when Constable David Maratse walked into the bar. I know because I watched him die. It was not an eloquent death, more of an afterthought, but it fit the time and place, and the mood. It seemed appropriate somehow. The bar was suitably dingy, the floor beer-tacky beneath the soles of my hiking boots. The walls were stained black with sweat and sorrow, the ceiling a sickly cream from the smoke of thousands of cigarettes each winter, and one more stuck in the gap between the policeman's teeth. I watched as he waited at the door, a nod to the barman, a glance at the body, and a lingering gaze towards the window banging in the wind, the murderer's exit. Snow lined the sill already, piling up as the body cooled, the pint glass still wedged in the man's throat. Maratse closed the door behind him and knelt by the side of the body, puffing at the cigarette between his teeth as he examined the wound, careful not to get blood on his uniform. The dim light cast from the pale lamps in the ceiling suggested he had not always been so careful, his jacket was spotted with all manner of matter – human or animal, it was difficult to say. This man, like all the men in the bar, was a hunter, he just happened to be dressed like a policeman. I placed my palm over my notebook and slid it across the table and into my lap. I needed to make some notes, for the record, for my book. And that's when he noticed me, Maratse, cigarette between his teeth, a frown on his nut-coloured brow, furrowing beneath the thick dark hair on his head.

"Did you see it?" he asked, his Danish clumsy but clear.

"Yes."

He grunted as he stood up. I made a note of his gait, slow but sure-footed, as he walked to the bar. I heard him say a name: *Aqqalunnguaq*, the name of the murderer. I rolled my tongue around my mouth, twisting and shaping it around the name, biting it into pieces – *akka* and *lung* and *wack*. The final letters seemed to get lost beneath my tongue and I realised I had missed something, as Maratse was leaving and the barman said something in east Greenlandic. Three men dragged the dead man out of the bar, as Maratse opened the door and twin beams of white light made the men blink as they stumbled outside, carrying the man between them in a manner that suggested it was not the first time they had carried their friend out of the bar, only this time it was the last.

The light was from the ambulance – a plain white transit with a wooden stretcher jammed between the wheel arches and assorted boxes left over from the last supply ship before the winter.

I pulled on my jacket, stuffed my notebook inside my pocket and followed the slick of blood across the bruised floorboards and out of the bar. I found Maratse waiting by the door of the ambulance as the driver helped the men secure the stretcher for the short trip to the medical station. The wind funnelled the snow into my collar and cooled my neck. It began to melt as I zipped my jacket, pulled up my hood, and tugged my gloves out of my pockets. Maratse, gloveless, bare-headed, watched me, and I walked over to him.

"Journalist?" he said.

"Writer."

"Book?"

"Yes."

"I read," he said, and lit a new cigarette. The flame from his lighter hesitated in the wind, and he cupped his hands to shield it, illuminating his bushy eyebrows as the flame reflected in the bowl of his palms, and the tip of the cigarette smouldered at the end, the tobacco revealed behind curling teeth as the flame bit into the paper.

"What kind of books? Crime?" I said and smiled.

"Science Fiction." Maratse tucked the lighter into his pocket. He nodded at the men as they returned to the bar and the ambulance driver shut the door and climbed in behind the wheel. Maratse began to walk towards his patrol car, a dark blue Toyota, engine rumbling. He stopped at the door and nodded at the passenger seat. "Want a lift?"

"Yes. Where are we going?"

"Hospital."

"What about the man who did it?"

Maratse lifted his chin and sniffed at the wind. "Where will he go?" He opened the door and got in. I slipped on the ice as I walked around the police car, clapped the snow from my trousers and climbed in beside Maratse. He shifted into first as I shut the door, the wheels pressing the snow into raised diamonds of ice with a squeal of pressure and escaping air. Maratse was quiet as we drove to the building he called a hospital – in Denmark it would have been called a clinic at best. He puffed on the cigarette. I resisted the urge to cough. He stopped the car outside the entrance, shifted into neutral and pulled on the handbrake. The car rolled, and he pressed his foot on the brake. Maratse grunted and pulled the handbrake higher until it clicked. He sat for a moment, and I waited for him to turn off the engine. He didn't. He rolled down the window and tossed the butt of his cigarette into a snowdrift. The fresh air was sharp; the sudden chill tickled my cheeks. The cold had a way of heightening the senses, and the stars pricking the black polar sky needled at my mind and I blurted out a request before I had the chance to think it over.

"Can I come with you?"

Maratse's breath frosted in the air between the seats as he looked at me.

"When you go and get him," I said.

"Aqqalunnguaq?"

"Yes. The murderer."

Maratse raised his eyebrows, and I grinned in my excitement – I had already learned, noted, and experienced the silent Greenlandic *yes*. Or so I thought.

"For your book?"

"Yes."

I waited as he fished another cigarette from the crumpled packet he kept in the top right pocket of his jacket. *Prince* was the make. The red wrapping and white lettering was unmistakable, and Danish. Maratse tucked the cigarette between the gap in his teeth. The missing tooth must have been pulled some time ago. It fit with what I had read about Greenlanders' teeth, and the lack of dentists in the Arctic. I watched as he flicked at the stub of the filter with his tongue. It seemed as though he might never answer, and the night air was sinking inside the Toyota.

"Never mind," I said. "It's probably too dangerous. I understand."

"Dangerous?"

"If he defends himself. I might get hurt. I understand."

Maratse frowned. "Aqqalunnguaq won't hurt you," he said.

"But he's a murderer."

"He's not a killer. But he will kill again."

"Who?"

Maratse paused to light his cigarette. The orange light softened his brow, and he said just one word, "Himself."

Justice, I thought, for the family, and I said so.

The tip of the policeman's cigarette glowed as he stared at me. He closed the window and curled his left hand around the door handle, applying just enough pressure that I heard it click, but he did not open it. Instead, he filled the cab of the police car with clouds of smoke as he puffed on the cigarette, lips parted, cigarette fixed in position. "You don't understand," he said, and got out.

"Wait." I fumbled with my door and stepped

out of the car. We shut our doors at the same moment. The clap of metal softened in the thick flakes of the growing storm. "What don't I understand?"

Maratse ignored me, extinguished his cigarette with a pinch and stuffed it into the packet. He kicked the snow from his boots at the door to the hospital and walked in. I slipped for the second time on the ice beneath the thick layer of fresh snow, picked myself up, and followed him. The Danish nurse frowned at me as I stumbled after the policeman. She glared at my feet as the snow pooled beneath my boots. Maratse wore a pair of thin plastic socks, blue and surgical, elasticated around the ankle. I found a pair – wet and gritty – in the bucket by the door and tugged them over my boots.

The nurse, grey-haired and tempered, said something about family only, but Maratse shrugged and nodded in my direction. "Special assignment," he said.

The nurse frowned again before leading the way into a small room with two windows, one in the outside wall lumped with snow, the other in the adjoining wall at desk-height; the light from the office filtered through it.

"They brought him in just a few minutes ago," the nurse said, as Maratse leaned over the man's neck to inspect the glass in his jugular.

"I know," he said.

I pulled the notebook from my pocket and licked the tip of my pencil – a habit and a reminder to take a beat, to observe and record.

"I haven't even called the doctor in Tasiilaq," she said. "Should I?"

"He's dead," Maratse said.

"I know, but protocol."

Maratse straightened his back and glanced at me and at the notebook in my hand. I stopped writing and waited as he looked at the nurse.

"His name," he said with a nod to the dead man, "is Frederik Lundblad, Aqqalunnguaq's brother."

"His brother?" I said and made a note.

"*Iiji.*"

The nurse reached for the clipboard at the end of the hospital bed and started making her own notes.

"Next of kin?"

"Margrethe, his wife."

"Lundblad?"

"*Iiji,*" Maratse said. He leaned against the radiator and stuffed his hands into the voluminous pockets of his jacket. His right hand twitched, rippling the blue-black fabric, and I wondered if he wouldn't rather have another cigarette. The flicker of his eyes towards the top pocket, and the tick in his cheek suggested as much.

"Children?"

"Three."

The nurse and I paused at the same time, and we both looked at Maratse, a man of few words and a wealth of information. I licked the tip of my pencil and Maratse caught my eye.

"You want to come?" he said.

"Yes."

"For a story?" he said and nodded at my

notebook.

"Yes."

I waited as he looked at the dead man. His eyes softened as he studied the wet swathe of blood on the man's neck, colouring the tattered hem of his t-shirt. I looked too, and, in the harsh white light of the hospital, I saw the details that had been hidden in the gloom of the bar. The man's face was pitted with what could have been teenage acne, but softened by the wind, the snow, and the sun. Another hunter, the creases, grooves and scabs on his nut-brown hands, confirmed it. I looked at his face. The bushy black eyebrows, the sporadic wisp of a moustache. The blood. Thick. Crusting in the warm hospital air. The man's clothes, tired and ripped, told another story. The next layer, beneath the surface, revealed the truth behind the romantic notion that was subsistence hunting. The bounty of the sea and ice was hard won. Little wonder Frederick and his brother chose to drown reality in cheap liquor. Except it wasn't cheap. Nothing in Greenland was ever cheap. Not really.

Maratse coughed, and I realised he and the nurse were watching me.

"Let me tell his story," I said, the words thick on my tongue. I cleared my throat and said, "Maybe I can give a percentage to the family." The thought slipped out.

"That's not your job," Maratse said.

"But the family," I said. I pointed at Frederik with the end of my pencil. I understood that most hunting families relied on the men, with government support. I also understood that life as a hunter and for a hunting family was tough. I just didn't appreciate how tough.

Maratse shook his head. "Aqqalunnguaq," he said.

"His brother? He murdered him."

"*Iiji*," Maratse said. He pushed off from the radiator and reached for the packet of cigarettes in his pocket. The smell of old tobacco leaked into the room as Maratse stuffed his half-finished cigarette between the gap in his teeth. The nurse protested, but he ignored her. He stared at me instead, waiting. It felt like a test, one I needed to pass if I was going to join him.

"Aqqalunnguaq," I said, and Maratse waited. "It's his responsibility now. He has to feed the family."

Maratse tugged at his utility belt and nodded. Just once. He walked past the nurse and me, stopping at the entrance to remove the blue slip-ons. I looked at the nurse as the elastic snapped once for the first, and then again, as he removed the second.

"You'll contact the deceased's family?" the nurse asked.

"*Iiji*," he said, and walked out of the hospital.

"I have to go," I said and slipped out of the room. I glanced at the dead man once more before struggling to remove the covers from my boots. Maratse flashed the lights of the police car once as he backed away from the hospital and began to turn. I stuffed my notepad and pencil into my pocket and stepped outside. The cold caught in my throat, as the snow brushed its needle edges against the surface of my eyes. I squinted into the snow, searching for Maratse. I turned my head at a squeal of deep rubber tread in the snow, as he stopped the police car beside me. The door opened, and I was enveloped in a cloud of smoke, as Maratse leaned across the passenger seat and beckoned me inside.

"Storm's coming," he said, as I shut the door and he accelerated away from the hospital. He grinned as I fumbled for my seatbelt. I gave up, and we powered along the road in search of a man that was not allowed to take his own life. Arctic justice, I thought. It's just not that simple.

2

Maratse said nothing during the short drive through the settlement. The Toyota's engine changed pitch in accordance to the grade of the road, and I listened to the alternating whines and growls as the snow flocked on the wipers, and the visibility narrowed to a single fan of glass that Maratse leaned forwards to look through. He stopped the car as a house loomed ahead of us and we got out.

The first breath I took was welcome, despite the snow plastering my hair and my neck. The policeman was a learned student of smoking, and his studies threatened to suffocate my research as I coughed and recycled the air in my lungs. Maratse ignored the sledge dogs as he trudged through the snow to the front door and I followed him, flicking my head to each side at the rattle of a chain, and the feral glint of eyes shining in the Toyota's headlights. The dogs seemed subdued, and I wondered if it was the weather or the death of their master. When I entered the house, I soon realised it was neither.

The woman who opened the door was prettier than I had anticipated. Maratse greeted her with a nod. He cupped his hand beneath her elbow, steadying her as he removed the can of beer from her hand. He kicked off his boots and guided the woman inside the house. They reached the sofa before I had finished untying my laces. She began to howl as I shut the door.

I understood nothing of what Maratse said, and even less of what she sobbed, but the faces of the children at her feet, behind the sofa, and peering around the door of the kitchen impressed me with their curiosity and calm. I watched them as Maratse talked. The oldest, a grubby boy with a light patch of skin scolded on his cheek, walked around the sofa and into the hall. Maratse flicked his eyes in the boy's direction, soothing the woman with the guttural q's, g's, and k's of the east Greenlandic dialect, all the while watching the boy as he dressed. A girl, perhaps three years younger than the boy, whispered past me and helped her brother buckle the huge belt – his father's, maybe – around the waist of the thin overalls. Maratse padded across the floor, away from the mother, and placed his hand on the boy's shoulder.

"*Eeqqi*," he said with a shake of his head.

The boy paused and then fiddled with the belt until Maratse pulled him into an awkward embrace, restraining the boy as he wriggled and kicked. The boy's sister retreated and his mother wailed at him, begging him to stop, I presumed.

I wondered at the boy's courage. He barely reached Maratse's elbow, and yet he was prepared to go and find his father's killer, to serve justice on his own uncle, and then I realised where we were, observed more closely the worn photographs peeling off the walls and the pervasive odour of dog, flesh, and fish. This was the house of a hunter.

KATABATIC

We were inside the killer's house.

The hairs on my skin stiffened, and I caught myself looking around the threadbare furniture towards the narrow stairs leading up a dark staircase to the first floor. I held my breath, only to gasp as Maratse released the boy into the living room and into his mother's arms. The boy straddled his mother, worming his arms between the cushions and her back, the cuffs of the oversized overalls rucking up around his arms. She flinched as the boy dug his knees into her ribs and sobbed into her shoulder. Strands of her long black hair, wet from her tears, wet from his, stuck to her cheeks, caught in his hair, pinched between his grubby fingers and the sofa. Maratse walked into the room and the girl followed. She stopped at her mother's knees and stroked her brother's back. Her siblings clustered around the sofa, touching it with tentative fingers. It seemed to me that the sofa connected them, grounded them, as Maratse talked to the mother.

She didn't blink for the minute or so that he talked. The breaks between his sentences suggested that he was explaining what was going to happen. I imagined him soothing her, telling her the steps he was going to take to take her husband into custody. It made sense to me. Maratse's tone betrayed a level of compassion that was perhaps typical of a local-born constable, someone she could trust to make the best of a really bad situation. His posture mirrored his words, relaxed, deliberate, soft, but when she blinked and spoke, he stiffened, as if he was caught off guard, and the situation was now wholly different, urgent even.

I stepped to one side, stopping as the woman flicked her eyes at me and then back to Maratse. He, in turn, glanced at her son, and his eyes betrayed a spark of comprehension. No longer did he wonder at the boy's actions, his choice of clothes, and his urgency. To Maratse, at least, it all made sense. Only I was left wondering as the woman finished speaking, smoothed her hair from her cheek with thin fingers, and clutched her son. She stared at the policeman, waited for him to respond.

Maratse took a step back, leaving the sweaty shadow of his stocking feet in front of him, as he sat down on a chair beside a bruised table at the window. He caught my eye and then looked out at the snow pillowing on the sill; the wind blowing it into a soft wave that was getting deeper by the minute. Maratse looked at his watch. He smoothed his fingers around the case, tapped the screen with a nail. He reached for the cigarette packet in his pocket, but stopped and scratched at his cheek instead. I pulled my notebook and pen from my pocket and sat down on the chair opposite his. The table creaked as I rested my elbows on the stained surface.

Maratse jerked his chin at my notebook and said, "What's it about?"

"I don't know yet," I said. I lowered my voice to a whisper, conscious of the woman staring at us. The sofa sighed as the children clambered onto it, closer to their mother. "What's going on? Where's the man?"

"Aqqalunnguaq?"

"Yes."

Maratse rested his arm on the table and folded his hand over his watch. "I was wrong," he said.

"In what way?"

"I said he would stay in town."

"But he didn't."

"*Eeqqi*," he said and looked out of the window. Maratse wiped his hand across his face and tapped his chin with his thumb. He looked at me, reached forward, and tapped his finger on the open page of my notebook. "Write this," he said.

"What?"

"I accept all responsibility for my actions…"

I wrote, slowing as I spelled the word *responsibility*.

"Sign and date it."

I did.

"Print your name. Write your address and CPR number, too."

I tore the page out of the notebook when I was finished. Maratse took it from my fingers and walked across the room to the opposite wall, the one with the faded photographs with curled edges. He slipped the page behind a portrait of the hunter and then spoke with the woman. She nodded several times, tapped the boy on the shoulder and whispered in his ear. The boy crawled off his mother's body, wiped tears from his cheeks and glared at me. He walked out of the room, past the dark staircase and into what I realised was the utility room, the light he switched on revealed the boiler and all manner of gear and clothing hung from drying racks, heaped on the floor.

"Go with him," Maratse said.

"Why?"

"You need better clothes."

I walked into the utility room, squirmed my stocking feet between fish-scaled trousers, sagging wool sweaters, assorted rubber gloves, and sealskin mittens. The boy tugged at my jacket and I unzipped it. He pulled at the cuffs and I let it fall from my body. He pricked me in the stomach and I removed my fleece jacket. He tested the thickness of my thermal top, rubbing the material between his fingers. The boy nodded and tapped my belt. I undid it and pulled off my trousers. The boy handed me a pair of thermal leggings, and I pulled them on, wrinkling my nose as I bent down to pull them up my thighs. The sweater was loose, musty and damp, but I pulled it on, the collar limp around my neck. I watched as the boy squeezed between the boiler and the oil tank. He grasped a pair of braces hooked around a pipe and dragged thick white salopettes into the light. The material bristled, and I felt the corners of my mouth lift in a smile as I recognised the fur of the polar bear. The odour from inside the legs of the salopettes was rich with the exertion of winter expeditions, but I didn't care. This was why I had come, to experience the culture at first hand; the smell was part of the experience. The thermal leggings scuffed against the felt lining and I grabbed the sides of salopettes, the polar bear fibres tickling my skin. It felt electric. I was electrified, and the boy knew it. He sensed my excitement and nodded, plucking at the fur with his fingers.

"*Nanok*," he said, and I recognised the word for polar bear.

"Yes."

He pointed at a smaller pair of furry salopettes hanging from a coat hanger.

"Yours?"

"*Iiji*," he said and grinned. I caught a glimpse of a rotten tooth before he said something else and presented me with thick wool socks, thin gloves with holes in the fingers, and a pair of sealskin gauntlets. I bundled everything under my arm and reached for my jacket, but the boy shook his head and handed me a thick cotton smock. It was stained with fish blood, decorated with flakes and scales. I tucked it under my other arm as the boy tried and failed to pull the braces over my shoulders. I dumped the clothes on top of the oil tank and tightened the braces as Maratse leaned against the door frame, his finger curled through the loop at the collar of his boots.

"Warm?" he said.

"Very."

"Good."

I reached for the smock and pulled it over my thermal top. "Will we be taking a sledge?"

Maratse shook his head. "No ice. We'll take a boat."

"Now?" I said and looked out of the window in the back door. It was black outside. The wind swirled snow down the street as far as I could see, and I began to imagine the ice in the bay, and the bergs in the fjord.

"Aqqalunnguaq left two hours ago. We can't wait."

"But we can't drive a boat in this."

"He can. We must."

"But the wind..." I said. I caught the tremor of excitement in my voice, tempered it with a cough. "I've seen the hunting boats. The bow will be flipped in the wind."

"That's why you're coming with me."

"As what? Ballast?"

"*Iiji.*"

I waited for Maratse to smile, for a glimpse of humour, recognition of the absurdity of the situation, but he didn't. His face was flat, his muscles still, only his eyes were active as they flickered from my face to the window and back again.

The boy pressed a pair of heavy rubber boots against my stomach. I looked down and gripped them. Then he handed me a heavy and hooded sealskin smock, cut with thick triangles at the front and back to protect the groin and kidneys. He said something to Maratse, and the policeman nodded as the boy brushed past him to join his family on the sofa.

"What did he say?"

"It's not important."

"I want to know," I said.

"*Eeqqi,*" Maratse said and shook his head. "You don't."

Maratse tugged on his boots, stepped over the gear on the floor, and opened the back door. The snow swirled around his feet as he stuck a cigarette into the gap between his teeth.

The door banged in the wind and Maratse held it as I pulled on the boots, grabbed my fleece hat from the pocket of my useless jacket and joined him at the door.

"Ready?"

"No," I said, and followed him around the house to the patrol car.

Maratse smoked as we drove down to the harbour area. I tried to think, but couldn't focus for fear of suffocating from the smoke of Maratse's cigarettes and the heat of the polar bear salopettes. It was only when we parked that I realised I had left my notebook on the table in Aqqalunnguaq's house, together with my death note.

3

There was a reluctant sense of urgency about Constable David Maratse as he changed his clothes at the back of the police car. I sat in the front, warm despite the shrill wind blasting cold air from the open rear door, cursing myself for the lack of a notebook, and yet surprisingly optimistic that I might survive the pursuit of the killer, Aqqalunnguaq. Despite what I had said to Maratse, the man was still a murderer in my mind; I had seen him commit the act. My optimism failed me as cars drifted down the hill to the harbour and the local hunters smoked and watched as Maratse took what he needed from the police car and slammed the rear door closed.

The watchers made no offer of assistance, protesting perhaps the effort required to catch the killer. But they were not silent, and even I, with no grasp of the language, understood the knowing nods, glares and gesticulations that punctuated the comments and jibes thrust in Maratse's direction. Not a few were aimed at me, but most were levelled at the policeman. Maratse ignored them and carried his gear in a holdall down to a row of fibreglass boats tied with frayed lines through rusted bolts cemented into holes bored in the rock. I got out of the car, shut the door, and walked across the snow to join him. The hunters followed.

I stood next to Maratse as he untied a line from the loop of metal in the rock and traced it back to a blood-stained boat, coiling the rope in his bare hands as he walked. I followed and waited at the stern. He threw the coil into the boat and reached inside his jacket pocket for a cigarette. Maratse still wore the police jacket, but he had changed his uniform trousers for salopettes like the ones I wore. He wore boots identical to mine, but I noticed fur poking out of the top and I guessed he had a layer of reindeer, or maybe even dog fur, inside them. My toes felt pinched by the cold as I realised I had yet to put on the socks the boy had given me. I sat down to put them on as the hunters arrived. Maratse lit his cigarette and waited for them.

I recognised one of the men from the bar. He stared at me and then started to speak in Danish.

"He'll die," he said. "Why are you taking him with you?"

Maratse stuffed his hands inside his jacket pocket and puffed on his cigarette. He paused to say, "You could always come, instead of him."

"Ha," the man said. I watched him shake his head. "I have a family," he said.

"So does Aqqalunnguaq."

The man shrugged and walked across the snow to stand next to the other hunters. Maratse looked at me and I hurried to pull on the last sock and my boots.

"Ready?" he said. Maratse pulled on a wool hat and fiddled with the strap of a headlamp until it sat snug above the rim of the hat.

"Yes."

"Put on your gloves. Put your hand under the gunwale."

"What about this?" I said and reached for a metal handle screwed into the hull."

"Broken," Maratse said. "Pull."

I lifted the stern of the boat as Maratse pushed the bow. We slid the hull across the snow towards the ice foot, the shifting boundary between the sea and the land. The tide was out, and we bumped the boat over the edge of the land and down onto the crust of ice skirting the coastline. The hunters followed, stopping at the edge above us for a better view. We were beyond the headlights of the cars and I felt dizzy when I looked at the black water and the black sky above it. The moon was hidden in the clouds and the snow on the ground could reflect little more than a grey pallor that did nothing to ease my concern. Maratse seemed unconcerned, and I wondered if his previous reluctance had been tempered with a need to get away from the spectators. He reached inside the boat and slung an M1 rifle around his chest. He grunted for me to move out of the way before lifting the bow of the boat and sliding it off the ice and into the water. One of the hunters slid down from the rocks and onto the ice. He gestured for Maratse to throw him the painter attached to a cleat at the bow of the boat. He held onto it as Maratse climbed over the side and worked his way to the outboard motor at the rear. I waited on the ice, acutely aware of the fact that I could count the number of times I had been in a boat this small on one hand. As for how many times I had been in a small boat at night in the middle of a snowstorm in Greenland? This was my first. Maratse lifted the rear of the outboard and then dropped the shaft down into the water. He looked at me and paused for a second.

"Last chance," he said.

"I know."

"You don't have to come."

"You'll do it alone?"

Maratse answered my question by flicking the butt of his cigarette into the water. I took a deep breath and grasped the boat, and lifted my leg over the side. The boat dipped, and I slipped, only to feel Maratse grip me around the shoulders, haul me into the boat, and guide me to the bench seat towards the bow. He sat me down so that I faced the stern.

"Better to look at me, so I can see if you get cold," he said, and nodded for the hunter to throw him the line. He coiled the rope beneath my seat, pumped the fuel line three times and then started the outboard motor. It took three vigorous yanks on the starting line before the motor sputtered into life. Maratse cut the choke and clicked the side lever into forward gear. We bumped against the side of the ice before he opened the throttle and pointed the bow of the boat west, away from the settlement, and deeper into the fjord.

The hunters slipped out of sight and I felt the black of the night press against the thick layers of clothing insulating me from the cold wind that picked up as we powered forwards. Chunks of ice clunked and knocked against the hull, as Maratse steered through the debris in the wake of icebergs calving in the fjord. I leaned over to peer into the water, curious all of a sudden as to how I would swim in my furs if I were to fall in.

"Don't," said Maratse.

"Sorry," I said, and moved back to a more central position. The boat levelled and Maratse pulled a cigarette from the packet with his lips. He lit it and watched me as I placed my palms flat on either side of the bench to steady myself.

"There's coffee in the bag," he said.

"Thanks."

"You might want it later."

"Where are we going?"

"There's a cabin in the fjord to the right. Aqqalunnguaq will be there."

"You're sure?"

"It's his cabin."

I nodded and then asked, "How long?"

"Two hours," Maratse said and squinted as the wind shifted and needles of snow flew horizontally into his face. "Maybe more." He turned the boat to the right and opened his eyes. The wind didn't howl as I expected, but the chatter of the outboard forced us to raise our voices.

"Why did he leave the village?" I said.

"Aqqalunnguaq?"

"Yes."

"*Qivittoq*," Maratse said. He exhaled a cloud of smoke as he watched my reaction.

"What's that?"

"It's what our ancestors did. If they did something to bring shame on their family, they went *qivittoq*."

"Went?"

"Left the village. Moved into the mountains. Lived like hermits."

"And they still do that today?"

"*Eeqqi*." Maratse shook his head. "Today they've learned how to commit suicide."

I shivered as the cold found the gaps in my pelt of armour, seeping down the sides of the rubber boots, two sizes too large, and around the cuffs and hems of my outer layers. I caught Maratse's eye as he studied me.

"If Aqqalunnguaq has gone *qivittoq*," I said, "will he still kill himself?"

"Maybe."

"But you're not sure?"

Maratse exhaled another lungful of smoke into the snow whirling around his head. The light from the headlamp caught the grey smoke and white crystals. The cloud dispersed above the boat and I watched it until it disappeared. My cheeks felt lumpy in the cold and I wondered for a moment if it would help if I smoked. I looked up when Maratse spoke.

"He was drunk when he killed his brother. We need to find him before he is sober. Before he starts to think."

"He must be thinking now," I said.

"*Eeqqi*. Now he is only acting."

"On instinct?"

"*Iiji*."

"And when he stops?"

Maratse closed a fist around an imaginary rope to one side of his neck and tugged it, tilting his head as he did so. He relaxed and concentrated on steering the boat, leaving me to wonder at the practical nature of Greenlanders. Suicide was, I knew, ingrained in their culture, almost legitimate. The government ran campaigns each year, but could not stamp it out completely, could not eradicate it. In some cases, suicide was contagious, resulting in a string of deaths and failed attempts. And, I realised, families of bereaved adults and children, lost in despair, powerless to bring back the dead. I thought of the little boy clinging to his mother, his sister consoling him, and the three other girls, five siblings in all, and one woman counting on Maratse to bring their father home. I decided I could cope with a little discomfort, could cope with the cold, in return for doing something worthwhile. But then Maratse cut the throttle, and the bow sank lower in the water.

"What is it?" I said and turned to stare into the black water beyond the bow.

Maratse shushed me and stood up. The engine idled and spat as he slipped the rifle from around his chest and into his hands. I followed his gaze and leaned forward to stare at a large floe of ice in the distance. The beam from Maratse's headlamp drowned a few metres in front of the boat and he turned it off. I waited for my eyes to adjust to the blackness, eager to see what it was that had caused us to stop.

I pictured Aqqalunnguaq lying prone on the ice floe, a rifle in his hand, waiting to deter anyone that might be crazy enough to follow him. Visions of Westerns floated into my head and I smiled despite myself, as I imagined the outlaws on the ridge waiting to ambush the sheriff's posse.

"And I'm with the sheriff," I whispered.

"Shh," Maratse said. I felt the boat shift as he moved, One hand on the gunwale, the other grasped around his rifle.

"What do you see?" I said as he passed me. The bow dipped, and he waved me towards the stern so that I might level the boat. "What is it?"

Maratse ignored me. The temperature of the air paled in comparison to the cold feeling growing in my gut. It was fear, and I fed it. I thought about how alone we were, a tiny vessel in a black sea, at least a kilometre from the land, several more from the settlement. If it was Aqqalunnguaq, if he did have a rifle, he wouldn't even have to hide our bodies. The sea would see to that. We were at his mercy.

Of course, what Maratse said next did little to reassure me.

"Can you see it?" he said in a whisper.

"What?"

"There." Maratse pointed with a straight arm, one o'clock from the tip of the bow.

"I can't see it," I said. "What is it?"

Maratse turned and grinned. "Bear," he said. "Large male."

4

I had never seen a polar bear. I was transfixed. The boat drifted closer to the ice floe, rocking as Maratse crawled over the centre seat and took hold of the tiller. He twisted the throttle and steered us towards another floe to the left of the one with the bear.

"Aqqalunnguaq isn't going anywhere," he said and pulled the dead man's clip from the throttle, killing the engine. The boat bumped against the side of the ice and all I could hear were snowflakes scraping along my collar as they dusted onto the deck of the boat. Maratse grinned and stepped out of the boat and onto the ice floe. He walked to the bow, took the painter and an ice pick, dug a loop in the ice and secured the boat. He beckoned for me to join him.

"Is it safe?"

Maratse nodded and pointed at the holdall beneath the centre seat. I gave it to him and he poured us both a small cup of lukewarm coffee. The floe spun gently as I crawled onto it to sit beside Maratse. He handed me my coffee and lit a cigarette.

"Do you see a lot of bears?" I said and took a sip from the plastic cup.

"*Iiji.*"

The snow dissolved in my coffee, and I drained the cup. It was surreal, the whole experience. Sitting on a floe of ice, drifting with the incoming tide, in the middle of a fjord, just metres away from a large polar bear, a male, its fur wet, sluiced into fingers of fur that dripped onto the ice. Maratse puffed a cloud of smoke upwards and when it was gone, I smelled something else. I smelled blood.

"He's eating," Maratse said and pointed a stubby finger at the bear. It held something beneath its paws, and I imagined a small seal being eviscerated with dense black claws, obsidian sharp, curved at the ends, the tools of the trade, the tools of the hunter.

"He looks thin."

"*Iiji.*"

The movement of the tide and the light wind allowed us to pace the bear rather than gain on it. I considered myself lucky and revelled in the moment, simultaneously engrossed and engaged in observation, while another part of my brain recorded the moment for the story taking shape in my mind.

"It's curious," I said, as I drew my knees to my chest and rested my chin on the salopettes. The fur tickled my skin as I watched the bear, and I chuckled as I realised that I could feel the bear as I watched it.

"What?"

"The bear, out here," I waved my hand in a casual arc to take in the black seawater and the distant shoreline, barely visible. "All alone."

"It's young," Maratse said.

"But alone, in such a vast…" The word caught in my throat as the ice floe dipped and the sound of water splashing behind us urged Maratse to his feet. I turned to see two small black eyes in a mask of white. A moment later and a second bear was on the floe, lifting its rear leg onto the ice.

"*Eeqqi*," Maratse shouted and drew the service pistol from the holster on his belt. "Go away. Go away." He fired a shot in the air as I scrambled to my feet. The flask slid across the ice as I kicked it; it disappeared over the side with a quiet plop. I reached after it and then checked myself. "Get in the boat." Maratse kicked me towards the boat and I slipped on the ice. I heard him yell at the bear again before he fired three times into its flank.

I twisted on the ice, pushed myself onto my knees and then slipped again, as the toes of the rubber boots found no purchase. My nose crunched into the surface of the ice and I tasted blood on my lip. I looked to my right and saw that the bear on the floe ahead of us was still, a great paw poised above the seal, its head pointed in our direction.

"The rifle," Maratse shouted. "Get the rifle."

I crawled for the boat, hurried and harried by the thought of trying to kill a large beast with small calibre bullets. The *huff, huff* of fetid air from feral lungs urged me on and I slipped over the gunwale and into the boat. I could see the rifle. It moved when I rocked the boat, the barrel pointing towards me. I lunged for it, curled my sealskin mitten around it and swung it up and onto the ice. The rifle was heavier than I expected and I couldn't hold it. It skittered onto the ice towards the bear.

"Fuck." Maratse fired six more rounds in quick succession as he lunged after the rifle. I rolled onto my side as the gunwale of the boat dipped with my weight and became caught under a lip of ice. I heard the metallic click and clack of the rifle as Maratse chambered a round. I could just see him beneath the bear as it reared. He rolled to the edge of the floe, as the bear crashed down onto the ice, pressing the boat down beneath the edge so that black water spilled over the side. I gasped as the water flooded into the boat, lifting the opposite side so that I was standing, and sliding into the sea beneath the ice floe. I flailed my hands for something to hold as Maratse kneeled, aimed, and fired into the muzzle of the bear. It roared as its lower jaw flew into the sea. Blood fantailed across the ice, spattering my forehead before I slid into the water. I heard one more shot before I sank beneath the surface.

I had forgotten all about drowning. The sight of the first polar bear, the coffee on the floe, the crisp whisper of snowflakes scratching my skin and catching in the fur of my clothing, had distanced me from the wafer of safety between life and death. It had dissolved, and I struggled with conflicting thoughts of lungs too cold to gasp, and my head grasped in a vice that pinched as it tightened. The sea freezes at minus 17 degrees Celsius, but I was going to die at less than 10. My fleece hat slipped off when I entered the water. That was what saved me, that and my long, greasy hair.

Maratse thrust his arm into the water and gripped my hair, yanking me to the surface so that he could loop the painter around my neck. My eyes bulged as he held me there, noosed against the edge of the ice floe. Maratse shifted position, hooked the toes of his boots beneath my arms and dug the sides of his feet against my ribs. I was heavy. He dragged me up onto his thighs, and then higher, releasing the noose around my neck as he grasped more of my body, just a few centimetres at a time, until I was lying on top of him and he rolled me onto my side. I spluttered a lungful of water onto the ice, heaving and wracking my lungs as I stared into the bloody half-face of the polar bear. It grinned with yellow incisors, a black snout, and three eyes – two lifeless orbs and a third blood-black hole a little to the right and above its left eye. The bear disappeared from view as Maratse rolled me onto my back and slapped at my face.

"Speak," he said, and slapped me again.

"Okay," I said, as I twisted my head to puke another pail of water onto the ice. Maratse crawled off me and I heard the metal side of the boat bump against the floe. I twisted my head away from the bear and watched as Maratse bailed the sea out of the boat. He worked fast. I forced myself onto my elbows, aware of something tugging at my ankle. It was the boat's painter. Maratse had anchored it to me.

"Do you see it?" he said.

"What?" I repeated the question, wrangling my lips around the tremors juddering through my body.

"The other bear."

I looked across at the other floe of ice. We were closer now. The see-saw motion of the fight must have given us enough momentum to close the distance.

"Yes," I said, as I spotted the first polar bear. Its head swayed as it sniffed the air. More blood. Fresh. More meat – fat for the winter. Fat for bones.

Maratse's feet sloshed in the remaining water as he moved about the boat, attaching the dead man's clip to the throttle, repositioning the fuel can. He curled his hand around the grip and yanked the starter handle once, then a second time, three times before it caught. The bear huffed and snorted at the sound of the motor, and then Maratse was on the floe. He grabbed me beneath the arms and dragged me to my feet. I wobbled beneath the weight of the water in my furs, and a frigid breath licked at my face.

"Is that wind?"

"Katabatic," Maratse said and grunted as he shoved me toward the boat.

"What?"

I slumped at the edge of the ice and Maratse lifted my legs over the side and dropped me into the centre of the boat. It rocked as he stepped into it and sat beside the throttle arm.

"Katabatic wind, from the mountains," he said. "Stay down. It'll be strong."

The huffing of the bear was lost in the roar and spray of the wind as it pressed against the bow of the boat, lifting it. Maratse kicked at my shoulder and urged me to crawl forwards. I shivered, nodded, and crawled, the sop of the sealskin gauntlets heavy in the water. I found a position that was sheltered from the wind, and pressed my cheek against a coil of rope, thankful to have my face out of the water, unsure if I was going to live, curiously unconcerned.

"Speak," Maratse shouted as the wind hurled spray and flecks of ice into his face. He fumbled for a cigarette and pressed it into the gap between his teeth. "Tell me a story."

"Sleep," I said, my voice slurred, my brain slowing. I had enough feeling to curse when he kicked me the first time, and again as he kicked me twice more.

"Speak."

"What to say?"

"Denmark. Tell me where you live."

"Gråsten."

"Where the queen has a castle?"

"Yes."

He kicked me again.

"I said yes."

"What's her name?" he said and cupped his hand around the cigarette to light it. "The queen." Another kick. "Her name."

"Yes, the queen," I said.

"Name."

"I..." I couldn't remember. It wasn't important. The coil of rope was important. The weave of the plastic, the frayed strands that cut into my cheek. That was important. Not the name of... Another kick, harder this time. "For fuck's sake," I said, and started as the bow of the boat dipped, the wind tore at my skin, and Maratse stuck his face in mine. I saw little but the orange glow of the tobacco burning at the tip of the cigarette, and then the smoke-breath, rancid and warm, in my face.

"Her name."

"Margrethe."

"*Iiji*," he said, and the bow lifted as Maratse leaped back to the stern and throttled into the wind.

Ice chunks thumped at the hull of the boat as Maratse steered us towards land and I drifted between his quizzes and kicks, my thoughts on the coil of rope, my pillow, and the cold comfort of the constable, like Argus, of the Ancient Times. My chill lips curled in a smile as I remembered the Jack London stories of my youth and gazed at the man at the helm of our vessel as he clamped the cigarette in his teeth and squinted into the wind, one hand on the throttle, the other stuffed inside his jacket. The cigarette was dead, but he sucked on the butt as he pushed us forwards, kicking me when the wind allowed it, all the way to the shore, until, with a crack of fiberglass, he jarred the boat into the ice foot where it swelled and heaved against the land, just a few hundred metres from a cabin.

"Up," he said and pulled me to my feet. Maratse reached down to untie the painter and pushed me forward to the bow, over the side, and onto the ice. The wind squalled from the mountains, down the fjord, and out to sea, and was forgotten for the moment, for there was smoke blowing horizontally from the cabin's chimney.

5

The winter vice pressing the sides of my head together tightened as Maratse pulled the sealskin smock over my head. He stripped me of the top layer of wet underwear and towelled my skin with his own thermal shirt. He pulled the wet sealskin over my head again and dressed himself. He nodded in the direction of the cabin, just over one hundred metres from the ice foot. The sledge dogs tethered outside the cabin were stirring; the rattle of their chains could be heard, just above the wind. Maratse guided me to a sheltered position behind a boulder, out of the wind, in sight of the cabin. He walked back to the boat and returned with the rifle.

"Can you use this?" he said.

"You want me to shoot?" The words trembled over my lips, part cold, part excitement.

"A distraction," Maratse said, and chambered a round. He handed me the rifle, pointed at the safety switch, showed me how to hold it, to tuck it into my shoulder. I thought of the polar bear, bleeding on the ice floe with a shattered jaw and a bullet in the brain.

"I don't think I can do it."

"Just shoot into the air. Above me."

"Where will you be?"

Maratse drew his pistol. He nodded towards an

area to the right of the cabin. "Over there."

The wind curled around the icebergs in the fjord, and I watched the whitecaps as they caught the light from the moon as the snowfall lightened. A deep cold settled on the land, pressing down on the layer of snow beneath us, lowering the temperature, and my confidence.

"I can't do it," I said and lowered the rifle.

"Then you'll die."

It hurt to frown, as if I was furrowing my brow within the ice vice, squeezing my head. "I don't understand."

"You're dying," Maratse said.

"I'm freezing."

"Same thing," he said and gestured at the cabin, "If I don't get you inside."

"Aqqalunnguaq is inside."

"*Imaqa*. Maybe." Maratse made a show of scanning the area above and on each side of the cabin. The snow reflected the light from the moon, stronger as the grey snow clouds dispersed and the cold black sky blistered with stars. Maratse pulled the wool hat from his head and tugged it over mine. He ran his hand through his thick black hair and grinned in the moonlight. "You wanted to come."

"Yes."

I turned away for a moment and studied the cabin. The walls were part sod, part boulder, part wood. It was an amalgamation of archaeology, modern nails buried into ancient turf. The roof was wood with bitumen panels tacked onto it, patched here and there with sheets of thick yellow plastic, the kind used to collect human waste in the settlements. Some of the repairs were recent, the council letters and logo on the bags still visible. The chimney, from which the smoke teased us with the promise of warmth, was crooked, rusted, but functional. The part of my brain unaffected by the cold admired the care required to patch and maintain the cabin with the few resources one had to hand.

I did want to come; I remembered. It was my idea, and this – I looked at the area surrounding the cabin, recognised it for what it was, an old hunting camp – was exactly what I wanted to see. I gripped the rifle, raised it to my shoulder for a moment, and then lowered the barrel.

"Yes," I said. "I can do it."

"Good." Maratse held the pistol at his side and took a step towards the boat. He stopped and gestured at the cabin. "Shoot over the roof," he said.

"And if he shoots back?"

"Shoot again." Maratse started to walk away.

"Over the roof?"

"*Iiji*."

I watched him all the way to the boat, calling out as he passed it. "When?" Maratse waved his hand, but I couldn't tell if it was four or five fingers he held up. I decided to wait until he was closer to the cabin.

The dogs twitched, one of them growled. I wondered that they didn't bark, but then recalled reading somewhere that they can't; they're too closely related to the wolf.

"Wolves, ice, and men." I smiled in spite of the cold and the situation. The adrenalin and excitement was kicking in. "About time," I whispered, as my teeth began to chatter.

I looked in the direction Maratse was walking. His black police jacket bobbed above the white polar bear salopettes, highlighted with the backdrop of snow, as if his legs and body had been severed at the waist. I watched as he closed on the cabin, approaching it from the east. The cabin faced west, towards the fjord. The small windows resting on splintered sills above the sod were dark and cracked. The cold sank lower still upon the land, and two more of the eight dogs I had seen fidgeted at the end of their chains.

"This is it," I whispered, and raised the rifle, pressing the butt into my shoulder.

Not for the first time, I was reminded of the Westerns I had watched as a child, and, later, as a young man. There was something familiar about the raw and solitary nature of the environment, the personal, intimate aspect of the hunt. We didn't track the killer to his hideout. We knew where he would be. I looked around. There were so very few options in the vast, unforgiving wilderness. Whereas dust and grit were synonymous with the majority of Westerns, here was only snow and ice. Horses had been replaced with huskies, wagons with boats. If I had been chewing tobacco, I might have been encouraged to spit. As it was, the excitement of the moment provided enough warmth to aim and squeeze the trigger. I fired a shot over the roof of the cabin, grinning at the recoil, chafing to fire again.

The shot roused the last of the dogs, shaking the

snow from their fur as they stood. I saw Maratse creep around the side of the cabin, but there was no response from inside. I wondered if Aqqalunnguaq was home.

"But where would he be?" I said and turned a slow circle within the shelter of the boulder. His boat lay on its side where he had dragged it up and over the ice foot. The snow was stained red by the side of it. A successful hunt, perhaps? So he had food. My stomach growled at the thought, and I almost thought I could smell roasted meat in the smoke from the chimney. I turned back to the cabin. Maratse was just outside the door. I fired again, chuckling as Maratse lifted the door handle upwards, pressed his shoulder to the door, and burst inside the cabin.

The black sky sucked the echo of the shot from the land, and all was still again. Even the wind was silent, exhausted of warm air. Content to rest while the sheriff confronted the killer and his deputy watched his back.

Except, the cabin was empty, and Maratse appeared at the door and waved for me to come. I carried the rifle in the crook of my arm and trudged through the snow. My socks had absorbed the water in my boots, but I couldn't feel my toes. I might have been worried if I wasn't so keen to get inside the cabin. Maratse took the rifle from my hands as I reached the door. He pulled me inside and told me to strip.

"Where's Aqqalunnguaq?"

He shrugged as he lit a candle and hung my clothes to dry over the line strung between the rafters beneath the roof. The cabin smelled of smoke and fat. Seams of old seal blubber sealed the rough grains and cuts of the wood floor, a natural varnish for the pallets harvested for the cabin. The roof was low, just a few centimetres from my head, and my clothes dripped from the line sagging beneath the weight. Maratse pushed me closer to the cast-iron stove, stoked and smoking in the middle of the room. He sat on the single cot jutting out of the cabin's northern wall, holstered his pistol, and stuck a cigarette between his teeth. I stood naked in front of the fire, arms folded over my belly as I twitched in the heat.

Maratse smoked. He didn't say a word until his cigarette was finished. He stood up and gathered several items of dry clothing scattered about the cabin. It seemed I was destined to wear more of the killer's clothes, as if donning his skin we might have better luck finding him.

"Not so far," I said.

"What?"

"Just thinking aloud."

I took the clothes from Maratse and pulled on Aqqalunnguaq's Long John underwear with a disregard for hygiene that would have startled my mother. But the sea had seen to that. Greenland did not tolerate sensitive souls, not if they wanted to live.

Maratse shuffled the few tins on the shelf and found a rusted tin of stew. He peeled off the wrapper, opened the lid, and placed it on top of the stove. The sweet scent of processed food caught in my nose and I swallowed the saliva triggered by the smell.

I found a pair of socks on the line, damp, but drier than my own. I put them on and sat on the cot. Maratse sat in the chair opposite me. Together with the cot and a three-legged table, it was the third and final piece of furniture in the cabin. He tapped his fingers on the arms of the chair. We listened to the pop of the stew bubbling inside the can.

"What next?" I said the first words not to shiver over my lips since I had fallen into the sea.

Maratse wiped a hand across his face and pointed out of the window at the dogs chained in front of the cabin. "Aqqalunnguaq has sixteen dogs."

"I only saw eight," I said.

Maratse nodded. "He has sixteen."

The pop and hiss of the meat distracted us both. Maratse used a grubby towel to wrap around the tin before spooning half of the contents into a dirty bowl. He handed it to me, placed the tin back on the stove and shined two spoons clean on the elbow of his jacket. We ate. Maratse finished first. He ate straight from the tin. He found a pan on the floor beside the stove and took it outside. I heard the clink of ice as he filled it from a plastic bucket beneath the window. The dogs began to howl as he chipped at the stubborn ice until the pan was full. He came back inside, shut the door, and put the pan on the stove.

"Tea," he said. "No coffee."

"Tea will be good."

I waited, anxious to hear the next move. The ice popped and cracked in the pan. Aqqalunnguaq must have collected the ice from the sea, debris from the icebergs calved from the glacier. I had heard stories of hotels on the west coast of Greenland, charging a fortune for whisky on the rocks, with glacier-old jagged cubes of ice fresh from the ice sheet. I ignored the thought of whisky and waited for tea.

I studied Maratse as the ice melted. His face was calm, black in the shadows, like the surface of the Greenland sea. Only his eyes were active, sharp and bright, betraying his thoughts. He knew what we had to do, I realised, but seemed reluctant to say it. The chair creaked as he stood up and made tea, dumping liberal amounts of sugar into chipped enamel mugs. I warmed my hands around the sides and sipped at the sweet liquid.

"Aqqalunnguaq has a camp over the ridge," Maratse said. "A few hours by dog sledge."

I took another sip of tea and waited. I was warm, and I admit that the thought of venturing outside again chilled my enthusiasm.

"You think he's there?"

"His boat is here. Half the team is gone."

"The dogs?"

"*Iiji.*"

"But we've no sledge."

"There's a spare behind the cabin."

That reluctant urgency again. It shone in the policeman's eyes while his body betrayed a penchant for laziness. I found the dichotomy difficult to fathom, and settled on the idea that Maratse was a consummate professional who was very, very good at relaxing. He shrugged and stood up.

"Finish your tea," he said. "Get dressed. I'll get the dogs."

6

A katabatic wind feeds off the land, growing in speed and energy as it descends from the ice sheet and accelerates into the warmer, denser air below. But the land, I reasoned, was covered in ice and snow, barren of life but for the foxes – the blue black and the white furred predators scouring the frozen wastes for prey – the snow hares, reindeer, ptarmigan, and … My thoughts froze as I struggled to think of life on the land, in the winter, and then I thought of us, Maratse and me, as we sledged up the slope towards the ridge. I tucked my neck deeper inside the sealskin collar of my furs. Maratse had pronounced them dry enough when he took them off the line. While I did not agree, I could sense that same reluctant urgency in his manner and his movement, as he collected the few provisions from the shelves and tucked them into the canvas bag he slung between the uprights of Aqqalunnguaq's spare sledge.

Unlike the sledges in the sledge district on the west coast of Greenland, the runners were deeper and narrower, with the thwarts higher off the ground. The snow fell thick and deep on the east coast, and the hunt often took the hunter into the mountains, whereas their western counterparts preferred the sea ice and the bounty below the surface. I leaned against the sledge bag, staring at Maratse's back as he snapped the seal hide whip to the right and left of the dogs on our journey away from the cabin, sledging the trail that led to Aqqalunnguaq's camp.

Maratse seemed equally at ease with the whip in his hand as he did behind the wheel of the Toyota, and I wondered, not for the first nor the last time, about the transition from one generation to the next. The television was introduced to Greenland just thirty years or so ago, and now the children had smartphones, their parents watched Blu-ray discs on flatscreen televisions, and the hunters often supplemented furs with synthetics, swapped sledges for snowmobiles. But the ice, the snow, the rock, the wind, the sea, boat, and sledge, these things were ingrained in each generation. Only in the capital and the south could one find Greenlanders that had never seen a sledge dog.

These thoughts entertained me, but did little to warm me as we ascended through the layers of deep cold pressing down upon the snow-blanketed land. So, when Maratse shushed the dogs to a stop and got off the sledge, I discovered the rapid warming that came as the result of pushing a sledge through deep snow.

"Take off your top," he said when I got off.

"I'll freeze."

"You'll sweat." Maratse hung his police jacket over the sledge bag and helped me do the same. He nodded at the uprights and told me to grip both of them and push as he led the dogs up and over the ridge at the head of the team. "There's no leader," he said. "They'll need encouragement."

"And we have to get to the top?" I said and looked up at the crust of white snow against a black sky illuminated in the moonlight.

"*Iiji.*"

"Okay. Let's get going." I shivered, my nipples hardening beneath the damp thermal top I wore above the polar bear salopettes. After the first few strides, the broad sides of the braces bit at them, and I slipped the straps off my shoulders. Maratse strode ahead of the team, swirling the tip of the whip in the snow with soft circular motions of his hand. The traces the whip left in the snow reminded me of worm casts on the beaches at home, but there was little life to be found between the rock and the snow this far north. I leaned into the uprights and pushed. The dogs panted, following their new master.

I noticed that Maratse favoured one dog in particular, letting it lean against his legs each time he stopped for a break. I watched from where I rested on the sledge, as he tickled it behind the ears, scratched the fur between its eyes.

"You like that one," I said, my voice thunderous in the deep quiet on the side of the mountain.

"*Iiji,*" he said.

"Is it a he or a she?"

"She."

She was slighter than the rest of the team; her paws smaller. I wondered why she didn't sink through the surface of the snow. She could not spread her weight in the same way as the larger males. Then I realised, once we resumed our trek, she seemed to sniff out the crusts of the snow blown hard by the wind, traversing them, leaving only the whisper of her pads depressed into the snow after her passing. Maratse did the same. Placing his feet as often as possible on the harder surfaces to avoid the tiring trudge of lifting one's feet out of the snow and onto the trail. I kept my feet inside the tracks of the runners, but I could still feel the sweat trickling beneath my armpits and pooling in the fibres of the thin fleece on my back. I tried to ignore it, to focus instead on breathing and pushing. I even closed my eyes, listened to the dogs panting, the sledge grinding the snow beneath the runners and the soft swish of Maratse's whip. And then all sounds stopped, and Maratse was at my side, pushing the sealskin smock into my hands and whispering that I should say nothing, as he took the rifle from the holster secured to the side of the sledge.

We had reached the top of the ridge, and there, less than two hundred metres ahead of us, was a small wall tent, with smoke rising from the chimney poking through a hole in the weathered canvas.

"He knows we're here," Maratse said. He checked the safety on the rifle and pressed it into my hands. "Same again," he said and walked in the direction of the tent. The bitch whined and bit at her collar until she was free. The dogs growled as she raced towards Maratse, ploughing through deep snow in her haste, until he stopped and she pressed herself into his legs. I watched as he crouched down to rub her ears before standing and pulling the service pistol from the holster at his hip.

A dagger of light sliced through the front of the

tent as a man, Aqqalunnguaq, peered out of the door. A shiver took me as I stared at his silhouette in the lantern light, and I felt alone all of a sudden, exposed. The rifle felt heavy in my hands, as Aqqalunnguaq let the door flap into place and the light was gone.

Maratse moved forwards, the bitch padding through the snow at his side. He stopped just twenty metres or so from the tent and I held my breath. This was when I imagined the sheriff would pull out the wanted poster tucked inside his jacket and call out the man's name. But Maratse said nothing. After a few moments, he urged the bitch forwards with a sharp command and a gentle kick to its rump. It ran forwards in a straight line to the tent. The snow to each side of her path exploded in showers of snow dust as Aqqalunnguaq's team of huskies felt the tremor of the bitch's paws on the surface and rose to greet it. The light sliced out of the tent again, and Aqqalunnguaq reappeared. This time, his silhouette was enhanced with a thin black line that lowered in an arc until it disappeared and I realised the rifle in his hands was now pointed directly at Maratse. I tugged the rifle into my shoulder, aimed above the tent and fired.

The muzzle flash blinded me for a moment, and I reached out to steady myself on the sledge, only to realise that it was gone. It bounced behind the dogs as they raced towards the tent in the excitement of the shot.

"Maratse," I shouted. "The dogs."

I blinked and shook my head. When I focused again, I could see that the sliver of light from the tent had grown to a crooked triangle, as Aqqalunnguaq whipped the door open so that it flapped against the side. He strode out in front of the tent, his silhouette fading as the canvas door slid off the side of the tent and closed. The dogs slowed as they passed Maratse and reached the rest of the pack anchored to the rock beneath the snow. They sniffed and squabbled as Maratse used the distraction to run east of the tent. Aqqalunnguaq raised his rifle and tracked him, and I fired again.

The dogs whined, and I imagined their confusion, they could not anticipate the next shot, and neither did I. When the snow to my right blossomed with a dark hole, and the crack of a shot rolled across the plateau towards me, I realised Aqqalunnguaq had fired his rifle, and that I was the intended target. I dropped Maratse's rifle and cowered behind a boulder, the surface cold and hard beneath my palms. There was another shot. It peeled through the black sky above my head and I promised – I might even have shouted – that I would stay down, that I would not shoot at him again. I slipped my hands down the side of the boulder and pressed my face into the snow, my head cooling as I turned to breathe. That was when I heard the first of two sharp reports. Quieter and faster than the rifles. The shots came from Maratse's pistol and they were the last I heard.

I lay there, my head in the snow, my heart thumping in my chest, for several minutes. I heard nothing, only the faint blister of snow across the plateau as a wind lifted off the ice cap and began to charge. I encouraged my heart to slow its beat with staggered breaths of frigid air, only to feel my pulse beat in my temples, and my breath catch in my throat at the sound of someone approaching with rapid movements.

The beat of feet through the snow slowed, and I looked up into the glaze-green eyes and black face of the bitch, Maratse's favourite. She pressed her face into mine and sniffed. I could feel her whiskers across my cheek, smell her fish-breath. I struggled, for a moment, to remember that it was a dog, not its ancestor, not a wolf. I lifted my head, and she recoiled, rump reared, tail twitching, head lowered upon her legs, front paws extended.

"It wants to play," I said, and the bitch fidgeted at the sound of my voice.

I shuffled into a crouch and lifted my head above the boulder to look at the tent. An oblong of light spilled from the door, and I imagined the canvas rucked around the tent poles after a struggle. The light played across a dark stain in the snow, and I stood and stared, bracing myself for the crack of a rifle, but nothing came. There was no one in sight. The plateau was quiet but for the pacing of a few dogs at the ends of their chains, and the playful bitch at my feet.

I took a step around the boulder, and then another towards the trail leading to the tent. The bitch followed. I stuffed my hands inside the sealskin, curling them within the tongue of fur that protected my crotch. The snow protested beneath my feet as I walked towards the tent. I could not feel my toes, but I lifted my leaden feet, one after the other, until I reached the sledge and walked between the dogs to within a metre of the tent door and the stain in the snow before it. It was blood, of course. The bitch curled past my legs and sniffed at it. I took a breath, and another step towards the door.

7

I reached for the door, curled my fingers around the stiff canvas, and drew it to one side. The lantern cast a dim light around the interior of the tent, the wick black within a flickering flame inside a smoky glass bulb. I blinked at the sight of Aqqalunnguaq, my first close-up since he thrust the pint glass into his brother's throat. His shoulders shook as he sobbed into his palms. The backs of his hands were traced and scoured with hard work. He sat on a reindeer skin and leaned against the cot at the rear of the tent. Snow pooled at his feet. I looked away from Aqqalunnguaq as the bitch squirmed her head around my legs, hesitant but curious.

"*Eeqqi*," Maratse said. He shooed her out of the tent with a single clap. That was when I saw the blood dripping from his fingers. I looked at the stain on the snow and back to Maratse. He nodded at the sledge knife, spotted with rust and smeared in blood. The blade was half-buried in the reindeer skin, about thirty centimetres from Aqqalunnguaq's feet. "He tried to slash his wrists."

"You stopped him?"

"*Iiji*." Maratse lifted his bloody hand.

I looked around the tent, saw Aqqalunnguaq's rifle on the floor beside Maratse, found a dirty shirt and tore off the cleaner of the two arms. I knelt in front of Maratse and bound the cut in his palm. It was deep. My fingers were slippery with the policeman's blood, spots caught in the fibres of my salopettes. I wiped my hands on the reindeer skin and sat next to Maratse. We looked at Aqqalunnguaq, and Maratse lit a cigarette with bloody fingers.

"What happens next?" I said.

He blew a cloud of smoke into the centre of the tent. The light dimmed, and I wondered if it needed more oil.

"It'll be light in a few hours. No sun. But light."

"So, we wait until it is light?"

"*Iiji.*"

"And then?"

Aqqalunnguaq slid his hands down his face, and I stared into the eyes of a haunted man. He looked just like his brother, only his moustache was thicker, his eyebrows bushier. His skin was more like hide, leathery and wrinkled far beyond his age. He stared back at me as Maratse talked.

"Aqqalunnguaq," he said, pushing his words around the cigarette clamped between his teeth, "is a proud man. This," he said with a wave of his hand around the tent, "is all he needs to provide for his family. He likes to drink. Too much. He knows this. He is mad for drink, and madder for it. It's his weakness."

Aqqalunnguaq and I listened. I was impressed with Maratse's flow, and then I realised he wasn't talking to me.

"But he cannot afford to be weak. No time for drink. He has to be strong now. I will help him."

Aqqalunnguaq's eyes flickered, and when he looked at Maratse, I saw a glimmer of hope. He looked at me, and a faint smile quivered across his lips.

"He won't go to prison?" I asked. Aqqalunnguaq shrank, and I saw the hope extinguished. I felt my stomach churn, and I wished I could pluck the words from where they hung in the smoke between us, but I could not. They were spoken. And yet, what kind of justice was this? The man had killed his brother, and I said so.

"What would you have done?" Maratse said.

"If I killed a man?"

"Your brother."

"I don't have one."

"A friend. What would you have done?"

"I'd be caught, punished."

"Locked away?"

"Yes."

"And your friend's family. Who'd provide for them?"

"If he had a family… I don't know. The State."

Maratse nodded, plucked the butt from his lips and pinched the last ember. "Lucky for you." He looked at Aqqalunnguaq. "He'll go to prison." Aqqalunnguaq paled and Maratse lifted his hand. "In Kangerlussuaq," he said, and Aqqalunnguaq sighed.

I remembered that Greenlanders who committed murder were often sent to prison in Denmark, isolated by language and culture, confined within walls so thick they could not hear the wind. I lifted my chin as the wind outside ruffled the canvas walls of the tent. How would a man of the ice survive in prison?

"Manslaughter," Maratse said. "The difference between prison in Denmark and detention in Greenland."

"You're not a judge," I said. "You can't choose his sentence."

Maratse looked at me. "It hasn't stopped you."

He was right. I looked at Aqqalunnguaq, the killer, the man, the brother, the husband, the father, the hunter. He was born surrounded by ice. The ice defined his way of life; it steered him and his thoughts. Surely, he would die on the ice, and he would have, if Maratse had let him.

Maratse shook his last cigarette from the packet, lit it, and handed it to Aqqalunnguaq. They shared it between them as the wind tugged at the tent guys and made the walls swell with gusts of increasing strength and duration. Maratse raised his voice and said, "I will run your team this winter and fish with your boat this summer. Your son will help me."

Aqqalunnguaq lifted his eyebrows and gave the cigarette to Maratse. He looked at me and grinned briefly, before looking at the policeman, waiting for him to speak.

"You'll give me the dog," he said. He pointed at the bitch lying at the entrance to the tent. The fur on its flank was white, the snow thickening, a quilt, insulation. "That one."

"*Iiji*," said Aqqalunnguaq. He reached beneath the cot and dragged a canvas rifle case onto the reindeer skin. I tensed. Maratse puffed on his cigarette. Aqqalunnguaq pulled a small calibre rifle out of the case and handed it to Maratse.

"*Qujanaq*," Maratse said and admired the rifle. "Good for seal." I relaxed when Aqqalunnguaq gave him the case and he slid the rifle inside it.

The walls of the tent creased and snapped and the wind howled around us, pitching from a hiss to a scream. The bitch retreated from the corner of the door snapping at its muzzle, and I caught a glimpse of the dogs curling thick tails across their noses as the wind buried them with waves of snow crashing upon their bodies. I looked at Maratse, and he nodded.

"We stay," he shouted.

"The cabin?"

"Too far."

Aqqalunnguaq stood up. He lifted a sealskin smock from the cot and pulled it on, nodding at the door, thrashing like a shark's tail caught in a feeding frenzy. "Fix the tent," he said. Maratse began to rise, but Aqqalunnguaq pressed him to the ground with a gentle hand on his shoulder. "*Eeqqi.*" He shook his head. "Your hand."

Maratse shrugged and sat down. He watched Aqqalunnguaq reach outside the door. The hunter dragged a metal pan full of ice inside the tent and thrust it at me. "Tea," he said, and pointed at a spirit stove on the ground beside the lantern. I nodded that I understood and shuffled over to light the stove. Aqqalunnguaq disappeared outside, securing the loose corner of the door to a peg in the snow. I followed his progress as he moved around the tent. With each guy he tightened the walls straightened, all but the side pointing east, the direction of the wind. That wall was cratered, the base of the bowl pressing inside the tent above the cot.

I set the pan of ice on the stove and warmed my hands beside it. Maratse crawled onto the cot and dozed. I heard Aqqalunnguaq's voice, single words hurled above the wind, and I pictured him checking his dogs, the sign of a good hunter. The ice melted and began to boil. I rooted through the hunter's box of provisions and found two enamel cups, a bag of tea, and another of sugar. We would have to share. It wouldn't be the first time. I smiled as I prepared the tea. Maratse began to snore.

I let the water boil, thinking that Aqqalunnguaq would return soon. When he didn't, and I had finished my tea, I turned off the stove and waited. The lantern dimmed and I let it, watching my shadow melt into the canvas as the wind buffeted the tent and drowned the policeman's snores.

I thought about life on the ice, about the katabatic wind feeding off the land, just as Aqqalunnguaq fed his family from the land. Reindeer meat, foxes knocked out cold in a stone trap, ptarmigan shot, plucked and roasted. The sea was even more bountiful, but there was a stark beauty about the lands – the dark granite, the black lichen, the snow, the ice. The lantern flickered, and the light clutched my shadow and dragged it into the darkness. I tucked my knees into my chest and curled my arms around them.

The shot, when it came, was almost lost in the wind, silenced by the gusting roar. It was the bitch that heard it. The scratch of her claws against the canvas door woke Maratse, and he rolled off the cot. The first thing he did was reach for the crumpled cigarette packet on the reindeer skin, only to crush it and toss it further into the tent. He spotted the tea on the floor, took a sip, swallowed and set the cup down beside the stove. He nodded at me, and then reached his hand beneath the canvas door and unhooked the corner from the peg. The snow clung to the sticky blood on his fingers. The bitch worried its way into the tent and between Maratse's arms. He cuddled her for a moment and then stepped outside. I followed.

The wind harried at us as we staggered past the dogs towards the ridge. We ignored it, feeling only the more insistent gusts as it spent its last energy storming down the mountain to the cabin and into the sea beyond it. By the time we reached the ridge, it had almost given up. The snow released from its katabatic clutches tumbled onto the plateau, brushing across the surface and around our legs all the way to the ridge, and the body half-buried beside the boulder where I had dropped Maratse's rifle.

Maratse held up his bloody hand for me to stop, and I waited as he walked forward, the bitch at his side, until he stopped and crouched beside Aqqalunnguaq's body. I heard a few words in east Greenlandic, and then Maratse reached out for the bitch and pulled her close. I took a few steps and stopped. I could see Aqqalunnguaq's face, and I could see the blood in the snow behind his head. I didn't need to see any more.

Maratse's offer of help had not been enough.

Either that, or the chance finding of the rifle had been too much, too tempting. What was it Maratse had said? Previous generations, when shamed, had hidden in the mountains, retreated from society and become hermits. But the generations to come had learned how to take their own life, like Aqqalunnguaq had done.

"With my rifle," I said. Saliva swelled in my mouth and I dropped to my knees and vomited, spattering the snow with thin tea and a sudden burden. The thought that I might even be responsible. I left the rifle there, by the boulder.

Did I imagine he might use it?

Never.

Did I wonder if he should?

I heaved another mouthful of tea onto the snow and wiped my lips with the back of my hand. I slumped onto my heels. A shadow slipped in front of me, and I watched as the bitch sniffed at my shame staining the snow. I felt a hand on my shoulder and looked up at Maratse.

"Okay?"

"Yes."

He nodded, and I noticed the rifle slung over one shoulder. The bitch padded around the snow, nose pressed to the surface, sniffing as she moved. We watched her in silence. The wind dropped, and I stood up.

"Ready?" Maratse asked.

"To do what?"

"Take him home."

I looked at Aqqalunnguaq's body and said, "That's what we came to do."

"*Iiji.*"

The twilight of a new polar day lit the plateau, and I glimpsed the cabin as the last gust of the katabatic wind broke against it. It had fed off the land; it had fed off the hunter, and now it hurled itself into exhaustion upon the black waves of the sea, much as we would soon do, as we carried the hunter home to his family.

Another Author's Note

I lived in Greenland for seven years. The sad fact is that I cannot remember exactly just how many people that I knew personally, and by association, that took their own life during the time I lived there. In the small Arctic community where we lived, my wife worked in the hospital, and I worked in the school, two of the most important institutions of any small, remote village or settlement. We saw our share of tragedies, but we were far less affected than the tight-knit families and communities who were the real victims of suicide in Greenland.

Katabatic, therefore, is based on experience, measured with a heavy dose of fiction. And yet, there is very little fiction in Greenland. Life is tough. The environment is unforgiving. Everything is extreme. It is little wonder then that everyday challenges often have or require extreme solutions.

How do you get the first supply ships of the year into the harbour when it is full of ice? The answer is dynamite.

How do you get from the island to the airport when the helicopter is grounded in a snowstorm? The answer is to drive across the sea ice in a delivery van.

The scenarios are endless, and the solutions are often very creative, as are the people.

The people of Greenland need a creative solution to eradicate suicide. Perhaps, in drawing some attention to it through my stories, I might inspire a thought, or an idea, that might lead to a solution.

I'll keep writing.

Chris
October 2017
Denmark

Printed by Amazon Italia Logistica S.r.l.
Torrazza Piemonte (TO), Italy

52338876R00041